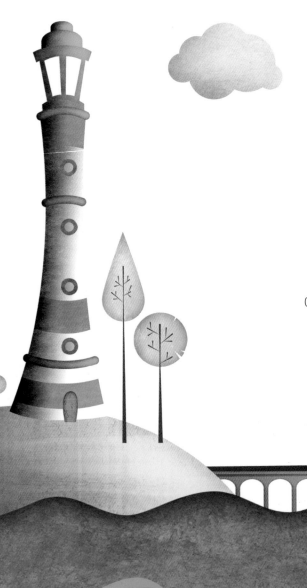

This edition published by Parragon Books Ltd in 2017 and distributed by

Parragon Inc.
440 Park Avenue South, 13th Floor
New York, NY 10016
www.parragon.com

Made in China
KOHL'S
Style Number 10574
Factory Number: 126509
9/17

The Fish with the Deep-Sea Smile

PaRragon

Bath • New York • Cologne • Melbourne • Delhi
Hong Kong • Shenzhen • Singapore

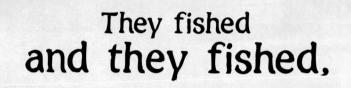

They fished
and they fished,

Way down in the sea,

Down in the
sea a mile.

They fished among
all the fish in the sea,

For the fish with the
deep-sea smile.

One fish came up
from the deep of the sea,

From down in the sea a mile.
It had blue-green eyes
and whiskers three,

But never a deep-sea smile.

One fish came up
from the deep of the sea,
From down in the sea a mile,

With electric lights
up and down its tail,
But never a deep-sea smile.

They fished
and they fished,
All across the sea,

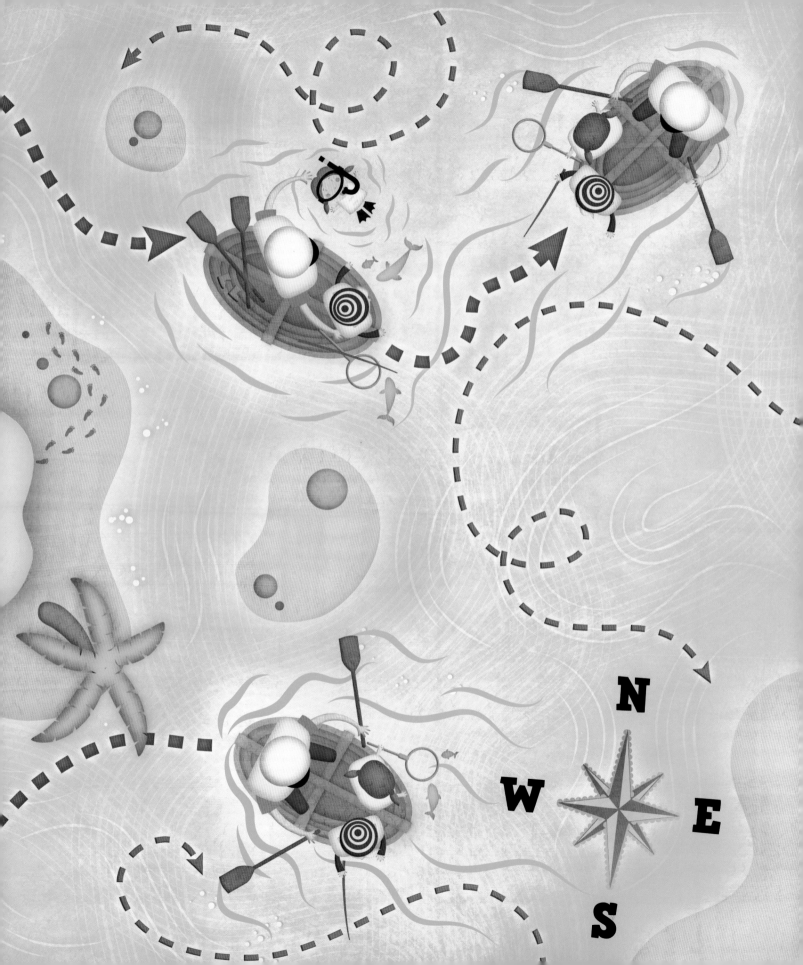

And down in the depths a mile.
They fished among all the fish in the sea,

For the fish with
the deep-sea smile.

One fish came up with
terrible teeth,

One fish with a long, strong jaw.

One fish came up with eyes on stalks,

One fish with terrible claws.

They fished all through the ocean deep,
For many and many a mile.

And they caught a fish with a laughing eye,

But none with a deep-sea smile.

And then, one day,
they got a pull,

From down in the
sea a mile.

And when they pulled
the fish into the boat,

He smiled a
deep-sea smile.

And as he smiled, the hook got free,
And then, what a deep-sea smile!

He flipped his tail
and swam away,

Down in the sea a mile.